For John Conheeney and Liam Tarleton,
the grandsons who inspired this tale
—With love, M. H. C.

To my friend Mary, who was born on Christmas Eve
—W. M.

ACKNOWLEDGMENTS

First of all, I wish to thank Jean Chapin, executive director of the Gunn Memorial Library & Museum, and Stephen Bartkus, curator of the Gunn Memorial Museum, for their invaluable help in providing important documents and artifacts, such as the beautiful antique wooden horse, essential to this story.

Founded in 1779, Washington, Connecticut, is a beautiful New England town, rich with history: The Averill Homestead, for example, has been home to nine generations of the Averill family since 1746. I am very grateful to Sam and Susan Averill for generously allowing us to use their historic home and farm for the setting of *The Magical Christmas Horse*.

Thanks also go to my friends in Washington who modeled for all of the characters within these pages. One might say that this book became a community project representing that enduring sense of family spirit in a small American town.

Lastly, I wish to thank our editor, Paula Wiseman, for her special insights, and art director Laurent Linn for bringing all the elements of text and images together in a wonderful Christmas package.

—W. M.

SIMON & SCHUSTER BOOKS FOR YOUNG READERS • An imprint of Simon & Schuster Children's Publishing Division • 1230 Avenue of the Americas, New York, New York 10020 • Text copyright © 2011 by Mary Higgins Clark • Illustrations copyright © 2011 by Wendell Minor • All rights reserved, including the right of reproduction in whole or in part in any form. • SIMON & SCHUSTER BOOKS FOR YOUNG READERS is a trademark of Simon & Schuster, Inc. • For information about special discounts for bulk purchases, please contact Simon & Schuster Special Sales at 1-866-506-1949 or business@simonandschuster.com. • The Simon & Schuster Speakers Bureau can bring authors to your live event. For more information or to book an event, contact the Simon & Schuster Speakers Bureau at 1-866-248-3049 or visit our website at www.simonspeakers.com. • Book design by Laurent Linn • The text for this book is set in Adobe Jenson Pro. • The illustrations for this book are rendered in gouache and watercolor on Strathmore 500 3-ply bristol board. • Manufactured in the Untied States of America • 1111 LPR • 4 6 8 10 9 7 5 3 • Library of Congress Cataloging-in-Publication Data • Clark, Mary Higgins. • The magical Christmas horse / Mary Higgins Clark ; illustrated by Wendell Minor. — 1st ed. • p. cm. "A Paula Wiseman book." • Summary: Eight-year-old Johnny, who lives in Arizona but feels a special connection to his grandfather's 265-year-old farmhouse in Washington, Connecticut, is overjoyed when his family spends Christmas there. • ISBN 978-1-4169-9478-7 (hardcover) • [1. Christmas—Fiction. 2. Historic buildings—Fiction. 3. Dwellings—Fiction.] I. Minor, Wendell, ill. II. Title. • PZ7.C5493Mag 2011 • [E]—dc22 • 2010013150 • 978-1-4424-3430-1 (eBook)

The Magical Christmas Horse

MARY HIGGINS CLARK

The Magical Christmas Horse

Paintings by
WENDELL MINOR

A Paula Wiseman Book
SIMON & SCHUSTER BOOKS FOR YOUNG READERS
New York ✦ London ✦ Toronto ✦ Sydney

THE FAMILY WAS GOING TO THE FARM FOR CHRISTMAS!

It seemed to eight-year-old Johnny Alvern that as far back as he could remember, all he ever really wanted to do was return to the house where his father had been born.

Johnny and his parents and little brother, Liam, lived in Scottsdale, Arizona, at the edge of the desert. Johnny's father was a famous painter, and people came from all over to buy his paintings of the desert. "Everyone has a heart home," he had once told Johnny, "and mine is here in the desert."

But the pictures Johnny loved best were the ones his father had painted years ago of the big stone house where he had grown up.

Johnny and his parents had visited Connecticut when he was three years old. Ever since, his grandparents had been spending the holidays with them in Arizona. Try as he would, the only thing Johnny could remember about being on the farm was riding on the beautiful wooden horse that one of his great-grandfathers had carved many, many years ago. His dad had told him that Johnny used to sit on the horse and pedal so fast that it was hard to catch up with him, and his grandfather had said it would always be Johnny's.

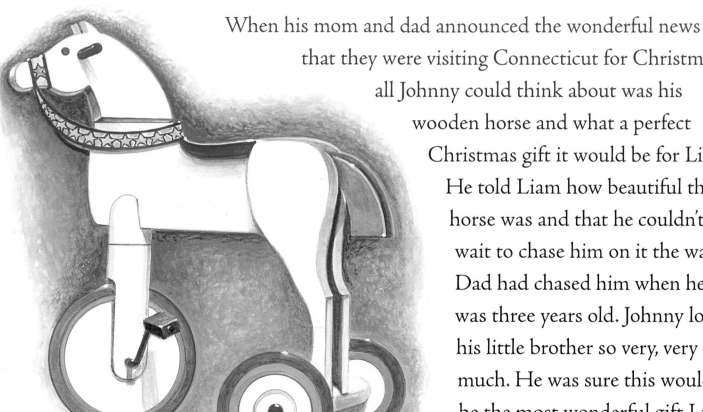

When his mom and dad announced the wonderful news
that they were visiting Connecticut for Christmas,
all Johnny could think about was his
wooden horse and what a perfect
Christmas gift it would be for Liam.
He told Liam how beautiful the
horse was and that he couldn't
wait to chase him on it the way
Dad had chased him when he
was three years old. Johnny loved
his little brother so very, very
much. He was sure this would
be the most wonderful gift Liam
would ever receive.

The last day of school before Christmas, they left. It was snowing when they drove into Connecticut, and Johnny was thrilled to watch the snow coming down. He thought of all the things that he couldn't wait to see. First was the great stone house that his family had lived in for two hundred and sixty-five years, with all its secret doors and fireplaces. It would be great to play hide-and-seek with Liam there.

When they arrived, the stone house was just like his father's painting of it. Johnny stood and looked at it for a long time even after the others went inside. Then when he did go inside, he ran through all the twisting, curving hallways, trying to see if he could remember any of them.

At bedtime Johnny asked his grandfather about the wooden horse. "Is it in the attic?" he asked. And then he shared his secret with his grandfather: He had told Liam about the wooden horse and promised it would be his Christmas gift to him.

His grandfather's voice softened. "Johnny," he said, "last year we lent a lot of antiques to be shown at a historical program two towns away. Something happened—the wooden horse was never returned. But I'm sure we can find Liam something at the toy store for you to give him instead."

Johnny didn't want to hurt his grandfather's feelings, but he knew nothing else would do.

Johnny remembered a book his mother had read to him when he was little, about a boy who wished for something so much that his wish came true. *I'll wish, and I'll wish, and I'll wish,* he thought, *and maybe someone will bring my horse back.*

That week he and his grandfather were always together. They walked all over the two hundred acres of the Alvern farm. His grandfather showed him the apple orchards and the hayfields and the vegetable gardens and the valley where the helpers were selling the Christmas trees. Johnny wanted to know every single thing about the farm: when everything was planted and when it was harvested, what was good weather for crops and what weather hurt them.

"You're a born farmer, Johnny," he said. "This will be yours someday, if you want it. It wasn't right for your dad."

Three days before Christmas, while Johnny's mother and grandmother prepared for the holiday, letting Liam help them, his father was working around the house fixing things from a list Johnny's grandmother had given him. Liam told Johnny how happy he was that on Christmas Day the beautiful horse would be waiting for him. But despite all of Johnny's wishing, no one had called to say the horse had been found.

The day before Christmas Eve, Johnny got up earlier than anyone else. Being very careful not to wake up his little brother, he slid out of bed and put on his robe and slippers. He had an idea. Maybe if he looked in the attic, he would find something else to make Liam's Christmas special.

The attic was very big and very cold. Johnny picked his way around carefully, but he couldn't see a single toy that might be right for Liam.

He was about to go back to bed when he looked at the attic trunks and decided to see what was in them. The first one was filled with pictures. One of them was of George Washington, and Johnny remembered that his grandfather had told him that the first president had stayed in this house during the Revolutionary War.

But there were no toys in the trunk. Making sure that nothing was disturbed, Johnny closed the trunk and went to another one. When he opened it, his mouth rounded into a big O. Inside was a military uniform like the ones he had seen in history books. He remembered that his grandfather's grandfather had been a military hero. This must have been his uniform.

As Johnny pulled the uniform up, his hands touched something else— something that couldn't be a uniform because it felt like it was made of wood. Carefully he lifted up the heavy uniform and, in the dim light, looked down. Underneath the uniform was the wonderful horse that they thought was lost. Johnny ran his hand over it, so happy to see it, so happy that on Christmas Day Liam would be able to sit on it, and Johnny would be able to chase him.

When he got a good look at the wooden horse, he was filled with disappointment. It wasn't the same horse that he remembered. The neck and three legs were broken, and the wheels were either missing or broken. The wood was cracked all over.

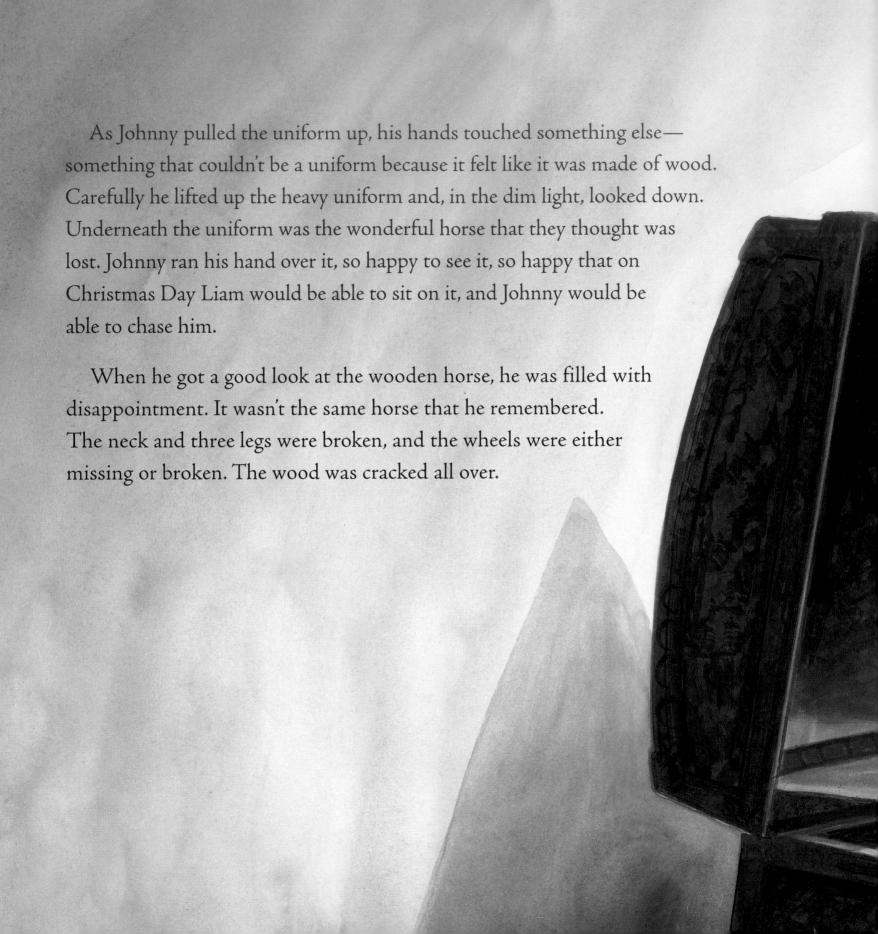

At breakfast Johnny's dad and grandfather could see that Johnny was very quiet. They asked him why. He told them what he had found and how disappointed Liam would be. "I have to break my promise," he said. "He can't ride on that horse now."

The next day, Christmas Eve, Johnny's grandfather said he was going to be very busy, so he asked Johnny if he would help the farmhands sell the farm's Christmas trees. Johnny loved spending the day helping people pick out trees, but he couldn't stop thinking about Liam.

All the while Johnny wished he could keep his promise.

On Christmas morning Johnny tiptoed downstairs very early. Santa had left many presents around the tree. But one thing stood out—the wooden horse. Both red knobs were in place, as shiny as when Johnny was little. The horse's body was gleaming white. The cracked legs were fixed and all the wheels were on the hooves. The tail was bright blue, as blue as the sky on a cold winter morning. The reins were silver and had gleaming gold stars painted on them. It was just as he remembered it!

"Grandpa and I didn't want to let you down, Johnny," his dad said, smiling. "Grandpa made new legs and wheels for your horse and new pegs so Liam can steer it, and I painted it."

"Liam will love it," Johnny whispered. "It's a magical horse."

"And we made something for you," his grandfather said. "We hope you think it is magical too."

It was a beautiful wooden Christmas ornament. The stone farmhouse was painted on it, and so were the fields and the woods and the barn. They were all covered with snow, just the way they were that Christmas morning.

"Grandpa carved this and I painted it, for you to have when
we go back home," his dad said. "If there's anything I'm sure of, it's
that this is your heart home. We knew you'd be glad to have this
reminder of it with you."

"Yes," Johnny whispered. "Yes." He looked out the window at the
snow falling on the trees and fences and fields. "When I grow up,
I'm going to live here always."

At that very minute they heard a squeal of delight. Liam was standing at the door of the living room. Without a word he rushed across the carpet and climbed onto the horse. "Chase me, Johnny!" he called.

Johnny put his beautiful ornament on the mantel over the fireplace. *Wishes do come true*, he thought, *especially Christmas wishes.*